BeastQuest

THE DARK REALM

→ BOOK THIRTEEN ←

TORGOR
THE MINOTAUR

ADAM BLADE

ILLUSTRATED BY EZRA TUCKER

SCHOLASTIC INC.

New York Toronto London Auckland
Sydney Mexico City New Delhi Hong Kong

With special thanks to Cherith Baldry
To Cameron and Brandon, true heroes

No part of this work may be reproduced, stored in a retrieval system, or transmitted in any form or by any means, electronic, mechanical, photocopying, recording, or otherwise, without written permission of the publisher. For information regarding permission, write to Working Partners Ltd., Stanley House, St. Chad's Place, London WC1X 9HH, United Kingdom.

ISBN-13: 978-0-545-20031-8
ISBN-10: 0-545-20031-8

Beast Quest series created by Working Partners Ltd., London.
BEAST QUEST is a trademark of Working Partners Ltd.

Text © 2008 by Working Partners Ltd. All rights reserved.
Cover illustration © 2008 by David Wyatt
Interior illustrations © 2009 by Scholastic Inc.

Published by Scholastic Inc., 557 Broadway, New York, NY 10012, by arrangement with Working Partners Ltd.

SCHOLASTIC, LITTLE APPLE, and associated logos are trademarks and/or registered trademarks of Scholastic Inc.

12 11 10 9 8 7 6   12 13 14/0

Designed by Tim Hall
Printed in the U.S.A.
First printing, October 2009

Welcome. You stand on the edge of darkness, at the gates of an awful land. This place is Gorgonia, the Dark Realm, where the sky is red, the water black, and Malvel rules. Tom and Elenna — your hero and his companion — must travel here to complete the next Beast Quest.

Gorgonia is home to six most deadly Beasts — Minotaur, Winged Stallion, Sea Monster, Gorgonian Hound, Mighty Mammoth, and Scorpion Man. Nothing can prepare Tom and Elenna for what they are about to face. Their past victories mean little. Only strong hearts and determination will save them now.

Dare you follow Tom's path once more? I advise you to turn back. Heroes can be stubborn, and adventures may beckon, but if you decide to stay with Tom, you must be brave and fearless. Anything less will mean certain doom.

Watch your step. . . .

Kerlo the Gatekeeper

HECTOR'S HEART POUNDED AS HE RAN through the forest. He had stayed too long playing by the stream, and now the moon was rising, purple and threatening. The angry red sky of Gorgonia swirled above his head. As he wove through the trees, the shadows seemed alive with danger.

Hector paused in a clearing to catch his breath and tried to see if any evil forest creatures lurked nearby. His heart beat faster as he heard a rustling sound. He darted behind a tree and pressed himself against the trunk.

Peering out slowly and cautiously, he spotted two young men crawling toward him. They kept glancing back fearfully, as if they were being followed. Hector gasped as he recognized the silver talismans that hung around their necks. These were worn only by the Gorgonian rebels who lived in the wood, where they plotted to overthrow the Dark Wizard Malvel. Hector's father had told him they were wasting their time. Malvel had always ruled Gorgonia; that would never change.

The two young men crept across the clearing and hid behind a tangle of ivy. They were now completely concealed. Still Hector did not dare come out from behind the tree. What were these two young men hiding from? Was Malvel on their trail? Hector felt his mouth go dry. What if the evil wizard found him cowering here, alone in the forest? Malvel would think he was in league with the rebels!

Then the ground suddenly trembled beneath his feet. Hector looked up to see a huge figure striding through the trees toward him, an enormous ax in his hand. The purple moonlight glinted off the golden blade as the fearsome creature swung the ax over his head and slashed through the trees that stood in his way. Hector tried to move, but fear had made his limbs useless.

A sob of terror escaped his throat. He had never seen this creature before, but he knew who it was: Torgor the Minotaur, one of the six evil Beasts of Gorgonia — and a loyal servant to Malvel.

The minotaur halted, looking down, and spotted Hector. His eyes narrowed. He was taller than the forest trees, and his vast body was covered with a thick, glistening pelt of coal-black hair. Two twisted horns rose from either side of his bull-like head. His arms swelled with muscles, and one huge fist was clasped around the ax's handle. The Beast tested the sharp edge of the weapon's blade with his thumb.

"Don't hurt me," Hector begged. The thought

of the ax swishing through the air toward him made him feel faint. The blade would cut off his head with one blow.

The Beast let out a threatening snarl, and saliva dripped from his jaws. Then he raised the ax above Hector's head.

"No, wait!" Hector shouted. He knew Malvel must have sent the Beast to hunt down the rebels, and he had an idea how he could save himself. "I'm not the one you're looking for." He pointed, with a trembling hand, to the ivy thicket where the two men were hiding. "Look over there." Hot shame engulfed him, but his only thought was getting away from the fearsome Beast and his deadly ax.

Torgor strode across the clearing and, with one swish of his ax, slashed the ivy into shreds, revealing the two rebels. They sprang up with cries of terror. For a moment, their eyes locked with Hector's, and then they bolted deeper into the forest. The minotaur let out a furious roar and raced after them.

Hector sank to the ground, trembling. At last, the thud of the Beast's footsteps died away. Only then did Hector dare to get up and head in the opposite direction, toward his home.

His legs shook and he stumbled over tree roots as he struggled toward the edge of the forest. He knew he had condemned two men to certain death.

"But I'm still alive," he whispered to himself.

CHAPTER ONE

THROUGH THE LION'S GATE

THE AIR TINGLED AS TOM STEPPED INTO THE Lion's Gate. It had appeared from the lake in Avantia after he had defeated Trillion the evil three-headed lion, but Tom had no idea what lay on the other side.

His horse, Storm, reared up. "Steady, boy," Tom murmured, patting the stallion's glossy neck. Storm rolled his eyes nervously but let Tom lead him forward.

Tom's friend Elenna walked at his side, with Silver close by. The wolf raised his muzzle and whined mournfully.

"We have to do this," Tom muttered through

clenched teeth. "Malvel is here somewhere, I know it!"

"You're right, Tom." Elenna's voice was steady. "And we have to rescue Aduro."

Tom stepped out of the gate. A flash of pure white light almost blinded him, and a shudder of energy shot through his body. He stumbled and had to hold on to Storm's reins to keep himself from falling. He heard Elenna cry out in shock, and Silver gave a high-pitched howl.

When Tom's eyes cleared again, he found himself standing in a wasteland. Flat, featureless ground stretched out as far as he could see. A few plants with limp, dark leaves and sprawling stems poked up through the gritty soil, looking as if they were dead or dying. A gnarled tree, bare of leaves, stretched out its twisted branches toward the four friends, and gray clouds hung low beneath a red, swirling sky. In the other direction lay desolate marshes, with reed beds and scum-filled pools.

Huge bubbles rose to the surface of the filthy water and burst with a gurgle and a foul smell.

"Ugh!" Elenna choked. "The whole place reeks. Has Malvel poisoned everything?"

Tom shivered and set his teeth against the damp, cold air, while Elenna pulled her shawl out of Storm's saddlebag and drew it tightly around her shoulders. "What place is this?" she asked.

"It is the kingdom of Gorgonia," a stranger's voice said from behind them.

They spun around to see a tall figure dressed in ragged brown robes, standing just in front of the Lion's Gate. Tom reached for his sword. Silver let out a growl from deep inside his throat, and Elenna grasped her bow, taking an arrow from her quiver.

The newcomer leaned on a staff of gnarled wood, staring at them. His head was bald, and one eye was covered by an eye patch; the other eye was a glittering gray.

"Who are you?" Tom asked boldly. He gripped his sword more tightly as the man shuffled forward. "Don't come any closer."

The strange man's mouth twisted in amusement. "Have I frightened you?" He gave a bow. "My name is Kerlo. I am the gatekeeper of Gorgonia."

"Are you a servant to Malvel?" Tom demanded.

"I am not," Kerlo said. "I do not serve any king or wizard. I simply watch the gate."

Tom wasn't sure he could trust this man, but there was no one else to ask for information. "What do you know about Malvel?" he asked. "I have to find him. Does he live near here?"

Again Kerlo let out a short laugh. "Find Malvel? You and your friend should go back to Avantia before it is too late. Gorgonia does not welcome foolish heroes."

"We are no fools. We're here to rescue my friend, the Wizard Aduro," Tom explained.

"And we're not going back until we find him," Elenna added defiantly.

Kerlo smiled, showing two rows of blackened teeth. "Very well, if you insist . . ." He stretched out a hand, pointing across the marshland with a bony finger. "That is the best way forward."

Then dark shadows began to swirl in front of the Lion's Gate, and the mysterious gatekeeper vanished into thin air.

Chapter Two

A New Quest

Elenna rubbed her eyes. "He's really gone! Do you think we can believe what he told us?"

Tom shrugged. "I don't know, but it's a start. We have to find Aduro." He stroked Storm. The stallion was trembling, and his eyes darted back and forth anxiously. "Everything will be fine," he murmured. He turned to his friend. "Are you ready, Elenna?"

"As ready as I'll ever be," she replied, "although this isn't going to be easy."

"I know, but don't forget that I now have the golden armor," Tom said, looking down at the precious relic he was wearing. "The powers it gives me will help us if we have to face Malvel."

As the words left his lips, a flickering light rose from the ground, enclosing Tom in a pale blue glow.

"What's happening?" he shouted.

He tried to punch his way out of the blue force field, but it would not free him. He felt his armor begin to vibrate. Then he realized that each piece was shaking itself free of his body.

Elenna threw herself forward to help, but as her outstretched hands touched the blue glow, she was thrown backward again.

"Stay back!" Tom yelled as the blue glow became a column of icy flame. He knew that Elenna could not save him from this magic.

When the flames died down, Tom's golden armor was gone. He was left standing in his ordinary clothes, grasping the sword and shield

that he had carried since the beginning of his first Quest.

"Tom!" Elenna gasped. "Are you all right?"

"I'm fine," Tom replied, staring down at his worn brown tunic and leggings. "But the armor's gone." Despair began to creep over him as he realized what he had lost. "What will we do without it?"

Elenna's eyes were wide with dismay. "Is Malvel really powerful enough to steal the armor from your body?"

Before Tom could reply, the air in front of him shimmered, and a figure began to form. Tom raised his sword. If Malvel was coming to finish them off, then both he and Elenna would fight until their last breath.

But it wasn't Malvel. It was Aduro! Tom lowered the sword in confusion.

King Hugo's adviser looked as if he were really standing in front of him. *But isn't Aduro Malvel's prisoner?* Tom thought. He stepped toward the good wizard.

"Tom, be careful." Elenna grabbed his arm. "This could be one of Malvel's tricks."

Tom looked hard at Aduro, and the wizard smiled at him. Tom suddenly felt as light as air. He would know that smile anywhere! It could not be faked. "Aduro, it really is you!"

Aduro reached for Tom's hand and shook it firmly. "Yes, it is."

Elenna let out a cry of delight and threw her arms around the good wizard. "We were afraid we'd never see you again!"

"But how did you escape from Malvel?" Tom asked.

Aduro smiled. "You both freed me."

Tom and Elenna exchanged a puzzled glance.

"How could we?" Tom asked, mystified. "We only just got here."

"When you recovered all six pieces of the

golden armor," Aduro explained, "you gave me the strength to get away."

A warm sense of pride filled Tom, but it ebbed away almost instantly. "I've lost the armor now. It vanished just before you came."

Aduro smiled. "Don't worry, Tom. The armor has been returned to its rightful place in King Hugo's palace. Its great power is needed elsewhere now."

Although Tom was relieved to hear that Malvel hadn't stolen the armor again, he was disappointed that he had lost his powers.

"Of course, you still have your special gifts," Aduro said, almost as if he had read Tom's mind. "They will always be part of you."

Tom looked confused. "But what about the —"

Aduro raised his hand, cutting Tom off. "My time here must be short," the wizard went on, "and there are things that I must tell you. Passing through the Lion's Gate from Avantia to Gorgonia was a test. You had the courage to do that, and now I know that you are both strong enough to face a new Quest."

Excitement tingled inside Tom as he realized that more adventures awaited them.

"What is it?" Elenna asked eagerly.

"Malvel has six more evil Beasts here in Gorgonia," the good wizard explained. "They must be destroyed before he has a chance to unleash them on Avantia."

Tom felt the cold touch of fear, but he drew himself up, gripping his sword. "While there's blood in my veins," he vowed, "I'll protect Avantia."

"So will I," Elenna added. "And we'll have you and your magic by our side this time, Aduro."

The wizard shook his head. "My magic cannot survive here in Malvel's kingdom. I weaken with every moment I spend in Gorgonia. I have no choice but to go to King Hugo's palace — now."

Tom gazed at him in alarm.

Aduro laid his hand reassuringly on his shoulder. "My thoughts will be with you on your Quest," he said. "I will watch you from the palace, and when I have the strength, I will appear to you in visions. But I will not be able to stay for long."

Even while the wizard was speaking, Tom could see that he was beginning to look haggard and weak. His firm grip on Tom's shoulder grew light.

"Go quickly!" Tom exclaimed.

The wizard raised a hand in farewell. Then in a swirl of robes and a sudden blaze of white light, Aduro passed through the Lion's Gate, back into Avantia.

Elenna stared out at the desolate landscape.

"How are we going to find these new Beasts?" she asked. "There is nothing here except wasteland."

"Kerlo told us to cross the marsh," Tom replied. "But that was when we were looking for Aduro." He gazed across the evil-smelling swamp, remembering how he had sunk into a similar bog when he was pursuing Soltra the Stone Charmer.

"Let's see what my magical compass can tell us," he suggested, pulling it from his pocket. It had been given to him by his long-lost father, Taladon, and had saved his life before.

The compass needle swung wildly for a moment and then came to rest on the word *Destiny*. The needle was pointing straight across the marsh.

"So this is the way to the next Beast," Elenna said, her eyes bright.

"And to our destiny," Tom replied. "Let's go."

CHAPTER THREE

MALVEL'S PLOT

TOM AND ELENNA STEPPED CAUTIOUSLY ONTO the edge of the marsh, trying to judge whether there was a firm path across. For an instant, Tom felt himself sink, then his feet came to rest on firm ground.

He peered into the distance, looking for a landmark. They needed something to aim for so they wouldn't become disoriented. Relief surged through him as he saw a cluster of buildings in the distance.

He turned to Elenna. "Even without the golden helmet, I can still see for long distances," he said happily. "I've spotted something!"

Elenna's face brightened with a wide grin. "What is it?" she asked.

Tom shaded his eyes with one hand against the angry red of the setting sun, and looked out across the marsh again. "It must be a village," he said. "Let's head for it." He sheathed his sword and took Storm by the bridle.

Elenna nodded and looked for Silver. The wolf was darting around excitedly but came to Elenna when she called him to her side. Tom mounted Storm, and Elenna scrambled up behind him. With Silver padding alongside them, they set out into the marsh. Tom guided Storm carefully, avoiding the pools of water that dotted the boggy ground.

They had not gone far when they heard a furious roar behind them. Tom spun around in the saddle, ready to draw his sword.

Brilliant white light was shining from the now-distant Lion's Gate. A second later, a dark figure burst through the gate and headed for the marsh, straight toward them. Tom caught his breath. It was Tagus the Night Horse, a good Beast and protector of Avantia, who had helped them to defeat Trillion the Three-Headed Lion.

"He must have followed us through the gate!" Elenna gasped.

Tagus plunged into the marsh. Tom slid down from Storm and splashed back through the mud toward the horse-man, waving his arms above his head. "No! Stop! Go back!" he yelled. He knew that Tagus couldn't understand what he said, but he hoped the Beast would understand his gestures.

But Tagus did not seem able to stop. He threw his head back and let out another roar, full of anger and frustration. He was trying to dig his hooves into the swampy ground, but some invisible force was pulling him onward, deeper into Gorgonia and across the marsh.

"I've got to try and block him," Tom said. "Keep Storm and Silver out of the way."

Elenna nodded, and guided Storm out of Tagus's path. The stallion was skittish but obeyed. Then Elenna called to Silver, who darted to her side.

Tagus was upon him now, but Tom did not move out of the way. The centaur reared, his forelegs striking at the air, barely missing Tom's head, trying to fight whatever was pulling him on, but his hooves continued to drag through the mud, and he was forced farther into the marsh.

Tom leaped forward and tried to grab one of the Beast's flailing forelegs, but it was impossible. Tagus's head thrashed to and fro, and he thrust out his legs as if he were trying to defend himself from an unseen enemy. His skin was shiny with sweat, and his eyes rolled back in fear. With a last roar of bewilderment and rage, he broke into a gallop.

Tom's hands clenched as he watched Tagus

race across the marsh. His hooves threw up showers of mud, but he went on galloping, faster and faster, until he was a speck in the distance.

Tom turned to Elenna. "Are you thinking what I'm thinking?" he asked.

"Something was forcing Tagus into the marsh," she said. "It must be Malvel."

"I wouldn't be surprised." Tom gazed out across the marsh. Tagus was now completely out of sight. Tom jumped into Storm's saddle in front of Elenna. "Tagus was heading toward the village. We have to follow him," he said. "Don't you see? There is a second part to our new Quest."

Elenna furrowed her brow and sighed. "I don't understand."

Tom gritted his teeth. "Malvel wants to send evil Beasts into Avantia once more. So he's pulling the good Beasts into Gorgonia. Without the good Beasts, Avantia has no defense!"

CHAPTER FOUR

ACROSS THE DEADLY MARSH

TOM URGED STORM FORWARD THROUGH THE marsh. The stallion tossed his head nervously but kept moving, picking his way around pools covered in green scum, through reed beds, and across tussocks of grass. With every step, his legs sank deeper into the swamp.

"This is no use," Elenna said. "The ground won't bear the weight of Storm carrying us."

"We'll have to get off and walk," Tom agreed.

Without Tom and Elenna on his back, Storm could now move more easily. Tom led him carefully, trying to find a firm track to follow. Elenna walked on Storm's other side, and Silver brought up the rear, mud splattering all over his gray-white fur.

Tom's feet sank into the marsh, and he felt cold water soaking through his boots. Clouds of flies rose into the air as he brushed past reed beds, and the mud he disturbed gave off a foul smell.

Elenna suddenly let out a cry of alarm as she tripped and ended up knee-deep in mud. "This is taking too long!" she exclaimed. "Malvel could be hurting Tagus while we're stuck here like this."

Tom gave her a hand to haul her out. He was afraid she was right, but all they could do was go on. No one else was able to help Tagus. Glancing around, he spotted a line of trees bordering the marsh in the near distance. Their branches were bare except for a few ragged leaves, and their twisted black shapes were outlined against the stormy red sky.

"Let's head over there and walk along the edge of the marsh," he suggested, pointing to the trees.

"The tree roots will make the ground more solid and keep our feet out of the bog."

"All right," Elenna agreed. "We'll certainly be able to move faster."

Tom was glad to lead Storm up a rough slope out of the swamp and toward the trees. Silver raced ahead, then stopped to shake himself vigorously, scattering mud everywhere.

"Hey, stop that!" Elenna laughed. "I'm muddy enough, thank you."

As Tom approached the trees, he saw that the small wood was thicker than it had looked from a distance, with a narrow path in its midst. Though there weren't any leaves on the trees, the branches crisscrossed and shut out the light.

Tom swung himself into Storm's saddle again. "Let's follow that path," he said decisively. "When we get to the other side of the trees, we should be able to loop back to the village and avoid the marsh altogether. It is out of our way, but I still think it will be faster than going across this bog."

"Sounds like a plan," Elenna said as she climbed up onto Storm.

Tom clicked his tongue to urge the horse into the shadow of the trees. But Storm refused to budge. He was trembling again.

"Come on, boy." Tom flicked the stallion's neck lightly with the reins. "We can't stay here."

Reluctantly, Storm began to move. Elenna called to Silver, but the wolf did not come right away. Instead, he stood stiff-legged at the edge of the trees. Elenna called again. Silver let out a chilling howl before following them into the forest, his head down and his tail drooping.

It was dark under the trees, with only a few thin beams of bloodred light finding their way through the tangled branches. The path soon grew narrower, and Tom had to guide Storm carefully to avoid sharp thorns on the bushes. Gnarled tree roots broke through the ground, waiting to trip them up.

The air was clammy, and Tom found it hard to breathe. "This is going to be our hardest Quest yet," he said. "But we'll come through — I know we will!"

Storm rolled his eyes and let out a loud neigh, as if he were agreeing.

"Silver hates this place," Elenna said, glancing down at her friend. The wolf was panting, his tongue lolling out. "But at least we're out of that awful marsh!"

Tom was about to reply when he felt something thin and sharp poke at his ribs. He looked down to see that a low branch from one of the trees was prodding him in the side. Tom pushed it away, but the branch immediately thrust forward again and poked him even harder.

"Hey, that tree just *went* for me!"

"It can't have," Elenna retorted. "Trees don't move. . . ."

Her voice died away as the sound of creaking and rustling rose from the forest, almost as if the trees were stretching their limbs. Above his head, Tom could see branches moving, though there wasn't a breath of wind.

"They're alive!" he exclaimed.

One of the branches swooped down. Elenna ducked. It retreated, but another branch attacked, its fingers raking at Elenna's hair.

"We've got to get out of here," Elenna cried. "These trees want to hurt us!"

↦ CHAPTER FIVE ↤

MALVEL'S MAP

Tom dug his heels hard into Storm's sides. "Go!" he shouted.

Storm fled along the path through the forest. Tom bent low over the horse's neck, with Elenna clinging on behind. Silver raced along beside them.

"Come on, boy!" Tom yelled, patting Storm's neck to encourage him. "Faster!"

On either side of the path, the trees bent over, reaching out their branches to snatch and claw at Tom and Elenna, the wood creaking with the sound of cruel laughter. Reaching down to his

shield, which was fastened on Storm's saddle, Tom rubbed the scrap of Tagus's magical horseshoe that was fixed there. The extra speed it would give them might just save their lives.

Storm's hooves became a blur as he thundered down the path. Thick, thorny bushes were closing in all around them, so Tom drew his sword. The skills given to him by the golden gauntlets helped him to hack a way through. Out of the corner of his eye, he spotted an ivy tendril snake out toward him. It tried to snatch the weapon from his grasp, but Tom was ready for it and slashed it away.

"Tom! Look!" Elenna cried, pointing over his shoulder.

Tom saw that they were coming to the end of the forest. He pushed Storm even harder and they burst out into the open again, beneath the swirling red sky of Gorgonia.

Gradually he slowed Storm to a walk. Glancing

back, he saw the whole of the forest moving, branches lashing to and fro in fury.

"What happened here?" Elenna asked, looking down at the ground.

All around them the earth was churned up. Trees had been uprooted and tossed aside, their roots twisting in the air.

"The forest has been ripped up," Tom replied. "I don't know why, but it's lucky for us. I thought we'd never make it out of there."

"Where's the village?" Elenna asked. "Can you still see it?"

He gazed around, looking for the landmark. Even with his magical sight, he couldn't spot the village he had seen earlier. Just flat land. "I'm not sure where we are," he replied truthfully. "Tearing through that forest has gotten us completely lost."

"How about Tagus?" Elenna asked anxiously.

"No sign of him, either," Tom said, shaking his head. "I just hope he hasn't been captured by Malvel." He pulled out his father's compass again, but this time the needle swung forward and backward without giving a clear reading.

"We'd better keep going —" he began.

But just then, a sizzling sound interrupted him, and a flash of red lightning struck the ground. Storm reared with a whinny of fear, and Tom had to struggle to get him under control again.

When the horse was quiet, Tom saw that something was lying on the ground where the lightning had struck. Elenna slid down from Storm's back and ran to pick it up.

"Careful!" Tom warned her, dismounting as well.

Elenna handed Tom what looked like a rolled-up piece of parchment. Tom shuddered as he touched it. It was greasy animal hide.

Holding it at arm's length, Tom and Elenna unrolled it.

"It's a map!" Elenna exclaimed. "I wonder if it's magical, like the map of Avantia that Aduro gave us."

Tom examined the map uneasily. The land it showed was unfamiliar, and across the top of it, in spiky black letters, was written GORGONIA. He glanced up at the stormy sky. "Did you send this, Malvel?" he shouted. "Do you think we're going to trust it?"

A familiar cruel laugh rang out. It was Malvel, though there was no sign of the evil wizard.

"We'll rescue Tagus!" Tom vowed defiantly. "And we don't need your map!"

"Ah, but I think you'll find it most useful," Malvel whispered, and then he laughed again, the sound fading on the wind. He was gone.

Tom and Elenna looked down at the map.

"Look, here's the Lion's Gate into Avantia." Elenna pointed. "That means we're in the southwest. And there's the forest, and here's the marsh."

Tom traced a line from the forest. "The village is not far from here," he said. "And look — there's a picture of Tagus next to it."

The tiny image of the horse-man suddenly became animated, rearing up and stamping his hooves. His head and upper body thrashed back and forth and side to side, as if he were trying to throw off invisible chains.

"Then that's where we must go to help Tagus," Elenna said. "Unless you think the map is trying to trick us."

"I don't completely trust it," Tom declared. "But it's all we've got, so we'll have to take a chance. If Malvel is leading us into a trap, we'll be ready."

He had begun to roll the map up again when

Elenna grabbed his hand to stop him. "Look! It's changing!"

Tom stared. Elenna was right. The edges of the forest and marsh were shifting, a tall and jagged rock face appeared, and a waterfall vanished. But the village stayed in the same place. All the landmarks were moving!

"Malvel's trying to confuse us," Tom said grimly. "He will try to make it as hard as possible for us to follow this map."

"Still, the map might help us if we're careful how we use it," Elenna said.

"Yes, you're right. Malvel thinks he can play games with us — but he'll find out he's mistaken. Let's get going."

Tom rolled up the map and stowed it away in Storm's saddlebag. As he and Elenna climbed into the saddle again, a purple moon appeared over the trees, shedding a threatening light over the ruined forest.

Tom urged Storm forward. He felt Elenna grip his waist and knew that his friend was as determined as he was. He clenched his hands on the reins.

"Whatever the danger, we'll face it," he said, "for the sake of Avantia."

CHAPTER SIX

TROUBLE IN THE VILLAGE

THE BLOODRED SUN OF GORGONIA WAS RISING again as Tom guided Storm along the rutted road that led into the village.

"At last!" Tom yawned. He was tired after traveling all night. "Maybe we can rest for a bit here and get something to eat."

"I don't know," Elenna replied doubtfully. "I don't like the look of this place. It's as if no one lives here."

"Maybe they don't," Tom replied, looking around at the crumbling stone houses. Their wooden doors and window shutters were rotting, and most of the windows were dark.

They continued on, passing more derelict houses. After a while, they could hear voices ahead. Storm trotted onward and they came upon a marketplace set on muddy ground. Ramshackle wooden stalls were set out in lines, and sellers were shouting out their wares.

"Fresh bread! Get your fresh bread here!"

"Ripe apples! Best ripe apples!"

"Pots to mend? Any pots to mend?"

Tom and Elenna dismounted and led Storm along the first row of stalls, looking at the strange piles of produce heaped up there. The turnips had two prongs, there were mushrooms growing on the apples, and the carrots were bright blue with feathery red tops. Everything was either dried up or worm-eaten. None of it was fresh.

"Look at this stuff!" Elenna whispered. "I wouldn't want to eat it."

"Nor would I," Tom agreed, thinking of the

plump apples and tasty pears that grew in the orchards of Avantia.

As they walked farther into the market, Tom noticed that the villagers kept turning to look at them. A stallholder froze as she was putting out her goods, sniffed the air suspiciously, then glared at them as they went by.

"What's the matter with everyone?" Elenna asked. "Why are they staring?"

Tom shrugged. "I don't know. Maybe they've never seen a horse as fine as Storm before."

"That doesn't explain why that woman sniffed!" Elenna's voice was indignant. "Does she think we smell bad?"

The woman wasn't the only one, Tom realized. Several of the villagers were sniffing now, as if they were picking up a strange odor.

"We can't smell worse than anything else in this place," Tom declared. "Just ignore them."

A large bearded man suddenly barged into Tom's shoulder, making him stumble.

"I'm sorry I —" the man began. Then he broke off, coughing and choking.

Tom tried to pat him on the back, but the man slapped his hand away.

"Don't touch me!" he yelled. "You have the stench of Avantia on you! You're vermin . . . you're a plague!"

Letting out a roar of rage, he launched himself straight at Tom.

But Tom ducked beneath the bearded man's meaty hands and skipped out of the way.

At once, the other people in the marketplace sprang forward, shouting and cursing. Their faces were twisted with hatred. An old woman waved her stick at Tom and Elenna and croaked, "You've got no right to be here!"

"Grab them!" someone else yelled.

They rushed forward but then halted as Tom drew his sword and swung it around in a circle.

"Keep back," he warned. To Elenna he shouted, "Get on Storm now!"

Elenna jumped nimbly onto the stallion's back. Tom was right behind her, but the bearded man leaped at him again and tried to tackle him to the ground. Once more Tom was too quick and neatly sidestepped him. The man ended up facedown in the mud.

Elenna had already set Storm into a trot, and Tom jumped up behind her.

"Go, Storm!" Elenna cried.

The stallion sprang forward into a gallop, hooves pounding through the mud of the street while Silver bounded alongside, yelping in excitement.

Tom looked back over his shoulder. Several market sellers were running down the road in pursuit. But Storm was too fast for them. They dropped back, and the sound of their shouting died away as Tom and his friends left the last houses of the village far behind.

They'd escaped!

CHAPTER SEVEN

A TRAIL OF BLOOD

AT LAST ELENNA DREW STORM TO A STOP. THE ground was covered with dead yellow grass and sloped down into a valley. A sluggish river wound its way along the bottom, with a few straggling bushes growing on the banks.

Tom looked back. There was no sign that anyone had followed them from the village. "I think we're safe," he said. "But how are we going to find Tagus? The map told us he was in the village, but they'll attack us if we go back there."

"Let's look at the map again," Elenna suggested, sliding to the ground.

Tom dismounted, pulled Malvel's map out of the saddlebag, and unrolled it, trying to ignore its slimy feel. The small figure of Tagus still stood beside the picture of the village.

"The map might be wrong," Elenna said.

Tom nodded. "Or maybe Malvel deliberately lied to us. Perhaps he wanted to lure us to the village because he knew the villagers would hate us."

Elenna pulled her shawl tightly around her shoulders. "We were lucky to get away."

Tom knew she was right. But now there was nothing to tell them where to go next.

"Hey, what's that?" Elenna interrupted his thoughts.

"Where?" Tom asked.

"Over there on the grass. It looks like a trail," Elenna replied, pointing.

Tom looked and saw a dark smear on the yellow grass, leading away over the crest of a hill. He led

Storm to it, while Silver raced ahead, sniffing the ground. He let out a small whimper.

Tom examined the dark red stains. He didn't need Silver's nose to tell him that it was dried blood. Then he felt his shield softly vibrating on Storm's saddle and saw that the scrap of Tagus's horseshoe was glowing faintly!

"Oh no!" Elenna exclaimed. "It can't be!"

"I think it is," Tom replied, his stomach in knots. "This blood must have come from Tagus."

Still leading Storm, Tom and Elenna followed the trail of blood. It led over the hill and along the top of the valley. Nothing grew there. They were once again trekking through a barren wasteland.

"There's something ahead," Tom said eventually, peering forward. His keen sight showed him a twisted tree and Tagus, their friend, lying among the gnarled roots. The Beast was moaning in pain and seemed to be straining against something that tethered him to the tree.

"It's Tagus — he's hurt!" Tom said urgently.

They hurried forward.

Tagus must have heard their approach. He turned his head as Tom and Elenna came up, his eyes filled with pain.

"Oh, look! Tom, that's horrible!" Elenna pointed at one of Tagus's hind legs. It was caught in the jaws of a vicious trap, and blood was still seeping from the wound. A thick chain tethered the trap to a root of the tree.

Tom clenched his fists angrily. "We're going to get you out of here," he told the good Beast, wishing the horse-man could understand.

Tom's presence must have soothed Tagus, because he stopped struggling and lay back against the tree roots with a shuddering sigh.

Elenna bent over the trap. "There's something written here. It says 'Torgor.'" Puzzled, she looked up at Tom. "What do you think that means?"

"It must be the name of the next Beast we have to face."

Elenna's face screwed up with disgust. "What evil is this? How can one Beast treat another so badly?"

"This is *Malvel's* Beast," Tom reminded her. "They're all evil to the core."

"Can you get Tagus out of the trap?" Elenna asked.

"I'll try. Lend me your shawl, Elenna."

She gave it to him, and Tom wrapped his hands in it, trying to pry open the jaws of the trap. It was no use. The trap would not budge. Drawing his sword, he hacked at the chain, but the blade didn't even scratch the metal.

Tom let out a shout of frustration. "It's too strong!"

"We've got to do something!" Elenna said, looking down at the limp form of the centaur. "We can't leave him like this."

Tom sheathed his sword again. "I can only see one option: We have to find Torgor and force him to free Tagus."

"Where should we start looking?" Elenna asked.

Tom gazed out at the horizon, searching for an answer. A little way off, Silver was sniffing at something in the grass; he looked up at Tom and let out an inviting whine.

"What have you got there, boy?" Tom asked.

He walked across to Silver. There in the grass was a faint set of bloodstained footprints, leading down into the valley.

"Look what Silver's found!" Tom called to Elenna, who had knelt down and was gently stroking Tagus's head. She jumped up and came to join him. "Torgor must have stepped in Tagus's blood."

"Another trail! We can follow it!" Elenna exclaimed.

Tom shook his head, his hand going to the hilt of his sword. "I'll follow Torgor. You should stay here and look after Tagus. Silver and Storm can stay with you, too. They'll help to protect you if Malvel shows up."

"I don't think so." Elenna pointed to Silver, who was waving his tail wildly, waiting for Tom to follow. "He's made up his mind to go with you. Look after him, and be careful."

"Don't worry, I will." Tom went back to Storm and unfastened his shield from the saddle.

Elenna sat down beside Tagus, putting a comforting arm around his shoulders, and waved good-bye to Tom. Part of him wished that she was coming, too; Elenna was a great friend to have in a tight spot. But he shook off this thought. Tagus needed someone to take care of him.

Torgor, you won't escape me, Tom thought as he strode forward, his eyes fixed on the trail of blood. *I'm coming to get you!*

CHAPTER EIGHT

FACING THE MINOTAUR

THE TRAIL LED TOWARD THE RIVER. EVEN though Tom was no longer wearing the golden chain mail, he was grateful for the strength of heart it had passed on to him. He gripped his sword and shield tightly as he braced himself to meet the Beast, and stayed alert for any unexpected sounds, but all he could hear was the wind sweeping across the barren hillside.

The dim light from the red sun made it hard for Tom to see, even with his extra-keen sight. Before long, the bloody footprints petered out, but Silver kept running frantically back and forth, letting out excited yelps as he picked up the scent of the Beast.

However, at the riverbank, the wolf seemed to lose the trail. He ran up and down, splashing through the shallow water and whining unhappily.

"What is it, boy?" Tom asked. "Where is the Beast?"

Silver let out a frustrated howl, and Tom guessed that the Beast had crossed the river. The water would have killed his scent; there was no way of following him any farther.

Tom looked back up the hill to where he could still see the twisted tree and the tiny figures of Elenna and Tagus. How were they going to help the good Beast now?

Suddenly, Silver let out a warning yelp. Tom turned around and spotted something flying through the air toward him at an impossible speed. He flung up his shield, just in time to fend

off a huge tree branch. In spite of the strength he had been given when he won the golden breastplate, he staggered under the force of the blow. Then his knees buckled and he fell to the ground. The branch thumped into the mud at the edge of the river.

Tom scrambled up, staring in disbelief at the enormous missile. Someone — or something — with incredible strength had just hurled it across the river. He gazed at the other side of the sluggish water, trying to spot his attacker, but could see nothing.

"Tom! Tom!"

Tom spun around at the sound of Elenna's voice. Mounted on Storm, his friend was racing down the hillside toward him.

"I saw what happened!" she gasped, jumping down from the horse. "I had to come. If someone is trying to attack you, then we fight together."

"Thanks," Tom said. "I —"

He broke off as Elenna's eyes widened. Twisting around, he saw that a pair of horns had appeared above the crest of a low hill on the other side of the river. They were huge, curved and shining, with wickedly sharp points.

"Torgor," Elenna breathed.

The pair of horns was followed by a bull's head, with eyes that reflected the scarlet of the sky. Below the neck was a man's body covered with thick black hair. He wore a leather belt around his waist, and in one hand he carried a giant ax with a golden blade. A ruby jewel winked where the axhead met the handle. He let out a roar of fury.

Tom's heart beat faster and his palms sweated as he reached for his sword. The huge Beast strode down the riverbank and splashed across the river toward him. Even though Tom knew that he still had the powers of the golden armor, he felt helpless in the face of such a monster.

But he stood his ground. He wouldn't give in without trying to fight.

"While there's blood in my veins," he vowed, "I'll defeat this Beast."

⇥ CHAPTER NINE ⇤

THE BATTLE BEGINS

TORGOR RACED OUT OF THE RIVER AND SWUNG his ax above his head.

"Look out!" Tom yelled at Elenna, who was quickly placing an arrow in her bow. As the ax whirled down toward them, Tom and Elenna leaped aside. The golden blade slammed down, shaking the ground so hard that they both lost their balance and sprawled flat on their backs.

Tom jumped to his feet, slashing at Torgor with his sword. But the Beast barely noticed the blows. Jerking the axhead out of the ground, Torgor headed up the hill, straight for the tree where Tagus still lay tethered. He swiped his ax through the air as he stalked toward the injured horse-man.

"He's going to kill Tagus!" Elenna gasped. "We've got to stop him!"

Tom launched himself up the hill. He couldn't believe how fast Torgor was. Even with the extra speed given to Tom by Tagus's horseshoe token, he had a hard time keeping up with the evil Beast's giant strides. He left Elenna and their animal friends far behind and reached the hilltop just a few paces behind Torgor.

The Beast stood over the trapped centaur, who was staring up at his captor with fury in his eyes. Tom was flooded with rage. As Torgor raised his weapon, Tom dropped his sword and shield, leaped up, and caught the ax by the blade. The Beast let out a bellow of fury and waved the ax wildly, but Tom managed to cling on, even though the golden blade cut into his palms.

As Torgor continued to whirl the ax around his

head, Tom felt his hands slipping. Finally, he lost his grip on the ax's blade and was thrown to the ground. The fall knocked the breath out of him. Gasping, he forced himself up onto his hands and knees. He could feel the hope in his heart failing. He just didn't have the strength to combat this Beast.

A short laugh made him look up. To his astonishment, Kerlo the Gatekeeper was standing in front of him, shaking his head.

"You're just like your father, Taladon," Kerlo said. "Too stubborn to admit defeat."

Tom's fury surged up again. "Leave me alone!" he shouted. What right did Kerlo have to criticize him or his father? Anger and determination gave him the strength to stand, to grab his sword and shield to attack the Beast once more.

An approving smile spread across Kerlo's features, and Tom realized that the gatekeeper had been deliberately trying to make him angry so he would get up and fight again. Was Kerlo on their side after all?

As Tom started toward Torgor, he heard a furious yelping and turned to see that Elenna was at the top of the hill with Silver and Storm. His friend was busy firing arrow after arrow at the Beast's back, but they bounced off his thick hide. Tom swung his sword around his head and jumped forward to hack at the Beast's muscular legs. But the Beast easily kicked the blade away.

Tagus tried to back away from the minotaur. But the horse-man's struggles only drove the teeth of the trap farther into his flesh, and a new stream of blood began to trickle down to his hooves. He kicked out with his forelegs, but the evil Beast was out of his reach.

Brave Tagus can't fight like this, Tom thought. *If only we could free him!*

As Torgor raised the ax above his head once more, Tom had an idea. He sprang between the two Beasts, just in front of the chain that tethered Tagus to the tree, and swung his sword at Torgor.

The minotaur let out a bellow of rage and swung the ax down with all his might toward Tom. At the last moment, Tom dove to one side. He felt the wind of the blade ruffle his hair and heard a loud clang as it struck the chain.

The links had parted. The chain was broken!

Tagus let out a roar. Rolling over, Tom saw him leap up, his hooves pawing the ground. Still trailing the vicious trap from one leg, he threw himself upon Torgor. As the two Beasts wrestled together, Tom felt a stab of pride. How brave the horse-man was! He surged forward to help, and rained blows on Torgor's back. Silver darted in and out, nipping at Torgor's ankles.

"Tagus, you can do it!" Elenna cried triumphantly.

The two Beasts churned the ground as they fought. Torgor wrapped his arms around Tagus's

body, trying to crush the life out of him, and lowered his head to gore the good Beast with his horns. As quick as lightning, Tagus reached up, grabbed the nearest horn, and twisted it.

A drawn-out cry of agony came from Torgor as Tagus snapped the horn away from his head. The minotaur instantly let go of the centaur, who dropped to the ground, panting. Torgor stumbled backward, then grew suddenly still.

"That's it!" Tom cried. His confidence came surging back. "Torgor's strength is in his horns. That's the way to defeat him!"

CHAPTER TEN

THE BATTLE ENDS

TOM RAISED HIS SWORD TO ATTACK TORGOR, but before the blow could fall, the Beast sprang into action again. He tossed his injured head and rushed at Tagus with a bellow of rage.

"Elenna!" Tom hissed. "Keep Torgor busy! Make sure he doesn't notice me!"

Elenna dashed forward and fired more arrows at the Beast, this time aiming for his face. The arrows seemed to sting Torgor like irritating flies; he batted at them and swung his head around to fix his red eyes directly on Elenna.

Tom dropped his shield but kept a grip on his sword as he climbed the tree. He worked his way along one of the branches until he was almost directly above Torgor.

With a loud battle cry that echoed across the deserted land, Tom leaped down from the tree and swung his sword at Torgor's remaining horn. The blade sliced right through it, and the Beast froze with his ax raised just above Elenna's head. The ruby set in the axhead flared with sudden light and fell to the ground.

As Tom landed lightly beside it, he bent and picked it up. His hands were bleeding from clinging to the ax's golden blade. He hadn't been aware of the pain until now.

"Tom!" Elenna gasped. "Look at Torgor!"

Tom straightened up. Red light surrounded Torgor, gradually hardening until it encased the Beast in a ruby prison. It reminded Tom of an insect trapped in amber. The Beast's mouth was still open in a roar of fury, but no sound came out.

"You did it, Tom!" Elenna exclaimed. "You defeated Torgor."

With a long sigh of relief, Tom knelt beside his shield and touched his wounded hands to another of his magical tokens: the feather of Epos the Winged Flame. At once the blood on his hands disappeared and the wounds closed up, leaving no scars.

At the same moment, Tom realized that somehow the leather belt Torgor had worn was now wound around his own waist. Six slots were positioned along its length, and it seemed right for Tom to place the ruby in the first of these.

"I wonder if this will give me another power, like the tokens in my shield, and the pieces of the golden armor," he said thoughtfully.

"Can you feel anything?" Elenna asked eagerly.

"No . . ." Tom began, then stopped as he heard a voice speaking inside his head. The voice was too weak for him to hear distinct words, but he could sense a powerful feeling of gratitude.

Tom looked at Tagus in astonishment. The Beast nodded.

"That's it!" Tom exclaimed. "Elenna, I know what Tagus is feeling! The ruby must help me to communicate with the good Beasts of Avantia."

A huge smile spread over Elenna's face. "That's wonderful!"

"Tagus," Tom asked, "is it true that Malvel has captured all the good Beasts? Are they all here in Gorgonia?"

Yes. Tagus's voice came through more clearly now.

Pain and anger flooded through Tom, as if Tagus were showing him what the other Beasts were suffering.

Tom exchanged a glance with Elenna. "This Quest has only just begun."

Suddenly, he became aware of his shadow stretching in front of him. A blue-white light was shining brightly behind him. At the same moment, Elenna exclaimed, "Aduro!"

Tom whirled around to see the good wizard standing under the tree. The gnarled trunk was visible through the wizard's body, and Tom realized it was only a vision.

"Well done, Tom," Aduro said. "Well done, both of you." He beckoned to Tagus, who limped toward him, his leg still in the trap. "I cannot stay long," Wizard Aduro went on. "I have little strength in this place, and I must use it to send Tagus back to his home in Avantia. Tagus, are you ready?"

The centaur nodded. Tom heard the word *farewell* echoing in his mind. "Good-bye, Tagus," he said.

"Good luck!" Elenna called.

Aduro raised his arms, and the blue-white light appeared again, flaring up as it transformed into the Lion's Gate. Through it, Tom could see the green plains of Avantia. A pang of homesickness resonated inside him, but he realized it would be a long time before he could return.

Tagus hobbled through the gate, but the moment his hooves touched the green grass of Avantia, the trap fell off his leg and he began to gallop. The terrible wound was healed. He raised a hand in a last farewell before racing into the distance.

Then the bright light faded and Aduro was gone.

Tom and Elenna turned to face each other.

"I'm glad we saw that," Elenna said softly. "I needed to know that Tagus was all right."

"Me, too," Tom agreed. "Meanwhile, we remain in Malvel's evil kingdom. We've work to do here."

"I can't help wondering where Malvel is," Elenna went on as she began to collect her spent arrows. "I'm surprised he hasn't turned up."

Tom suppressed a shudder. He didn't want to think what the evil wizard might be up to.

"Never mind Malvel," he replied resolutely. "We have more Beasts to free."

"I wonder which one we will find next," Elenna said.

Tom looked around for their animal friends. Storm was waiting a little way down the hill, while Silver had padded up to the ruby prison surrounding Torgor and was sniffing curiously at its base.

Tom recovered his shield and went over to tie it onto Storm's saddle. Then he saw that the feather he had received from Epos the Winged Flame was shining and vibrating softly.

"That's it," he said. "The next Beast we have to save is Epos."

He turned and looked out across the barren hills of this strange new kingdom. Somewhere out there, another good Beast needed their help.

Whatever it took, he, Elenna, Storm, and Silver would rise to the challenge!